W9-CNC-313

BEDTIME for BABY SHARK
Doo Doo Doo Doo Doo Doo

A LA CAMA, BEBÉ TIBURÓN
Duu Duu Duu Duu Duu Duu

Art by / Arte de
John John Bajet

Scholastic Inc.

Originally published in English as *Bedtime for Baby Shark Doo Doo Doo Doo Doo Doo*

Copyright © 2019 by Scholastic Inc.
Translation copyright © 2020 by Scholastic Inc.
Adapted from the song, "Baby Shark."

All rights reserved. Published by Scholastic Inc., *Publishers since 1920*.
SCHOLASTIC, SCHOLASTIC EN ESPAÑOL, and associated logos are trademarks and/or
registered trademarks of Scholastic Inc.

The publisher does not have any control over and does not assume any responsibility
for author or third-party websites or their content.

No part of this publication may be reproduced, stored in a retrieval system, or transmitted in any form or
by any means, electronic, mechanical, photocopying, recording, or otherwise. For information regarding
permission, write to Scholastic Inc., Attention:
Permissions Department, 557 Broadway, New York, NY 10012.

ISBN 978-1-338-63099-2

10 9 8 7 6 5 4 3 2   20 21 22 23 24

Printed in the U.S.A.   40
First Spanish printing, 2020
Designed by Doan Buu

R0459302788

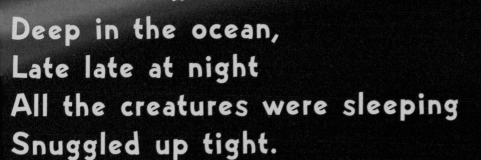

Deep in the ocean,
Late late at night
All the creatures were sleeping
Snuggled up tight.

The minnows were snoozing
And the whales snored deep.
But one baby shark . . .
Would NOT go to sleep.

Muy tarde en la noche,
En el fondo del mar,
Todas las criaturas dormían
Tranquilamente en su hogar.

Los pececillos soñaban,
Las ballenas roncaban sin cesar.
Pero un bebé tiburón...
NO se quería acostar.

Brush your teeth, doo doo doo doo doo doo.
Brush your teeth, doo doo doo doo doo doo.
Lávate los dientes, duu duu duu duu duu duu.
Lávate los dientes, duu duu duu duu duu duu.

Brush your teeth, doo doo doo doo doo doo.
BRUSH YOUR TEETH!
Lávate los dientes, duu duu duu duu duu duu.
¡LÁVATE LOS DIENTES!

Take a bath, doo doo doo doo doo doo.
Take a bath, doo doo doo doo doo doo.
Báñate, duu duu duu duu duu duu.
Báñate, duu duu duu duu duu duu.

Jammies on, doo doo doo doo doo doo.
Jammies on, doo doo doo doo doo doo.
Ponte el pijama, duu duu duu duu duu duu.
Ponte el pijama, duu duu duu duu duu duu.

Jammies on, doo doo doo doo doo doo.
JAMMIES ON!

Ponte el pijama, duu duu duu duu duu duu.
¡PONTE EL PIJAMA!

Read a book, doo doo doo doo doo doo.
Read a book, doo doo doo doo doo doo.
Lee un libro, duu duu duu duu duu duu.
Lee un libro, duu duu duu duu duu duu.

SHARK TALES
CUENTOS DE
TIBURONES

Read a book, doo doo doo doo doo doo.
READ A BOOK!
Lee un libro, duu duu duu duu duu duu.
¡LEE UN LIBRO!

Night-light on, doo doo doo doo doo doo.
Night-light on, doo doo doo doo doo doo.
Prende la lamparita, duu duu duu duu duu duu.
Prende la lamparita, duu duu duu duu duu duu.

Toss and turn, doo doo doo doo doo doo.
Toss and turn, doo doo doo doo doo doo.
Para acá y para allá, duu duu duu duu duu duu.
Para acá y para allá, duu duu duu duu duu duu.

Toss and turn, doo doo doo doo doo doo.
TOSS AND TURN!
Para acá y para allá, duu duu duu duu duu duu.
¡PARA ACÁ Y PARA ALLÁ!

Run and hide, doo doo doo doo doo doo.
Run and hide, doo doo doo doo doo doo.
Corre a esconderte, duu duu duu duu duu duu.
Corre a esconderte, duu duu duu duu duu duu.

Run and hide, doo doo doo doo doo doo.
RUN AND HIDE!
Corre a esconderte, duu duu duu duu duu duu.
¡CORRE A ESCONDERTE!

No more tricks, doo doo doo doo doo doo.
No more tricks, doo doo doo doo doo doo.
No más trucos, duu duu duu duu duu duu.
No más trucos, duu duu duu duu duu duu.

No more tricks, doo doo doo doo doo doo.
NO MORE TRICKS!
No más trucos, duu duu duu duu duu duu.
¡NO MÁS TRUCOS!

All tucked in, doo doo doo doo doo doo.
All tucked in, doo doo doo doo doo doo.
Métete en la cama, duu duu duu duu duu duu.
Métete en la cama, duu duu duu duu duu duu.

All tucked in, doo doo doo doo doo doo.

ALL TUCKED IN!

Métete en la cama, duu duu duu duu duu duu.

¡MÉTETE EN LA CAMA!

Off to sleep, doo doo doo doo doo doo.
Off to sleep, doo doo doo doo doo doo.
A dormir, duu duu duu duu duu duu.
A dormir, duu duu duu duu duu duu.

Off to sleep, doo doo doo doo doo doo.
OFF TO SLEEP!
SWEET DREAMS, BABY SHARK!
A dormir, duu duu duu duu duu duu.
¡A DORMIR!
¡FELICES SUEÑOS, BEBÉ TIBURÓN!

BABY SHARK BEDTIME DANCE! ♫ ¡EL BAILE DE BEBÉ TIBURÓN!

Move hand up and down in front of your mouth like a toothbrush.

BRUSH YOUR TEETH!  **¡LÁVATE LOS DIENTES!**

Mueve la mano frente a la boca como cepillándote los dientes.

Wave a hand behind your head like a scrub brush.

TAKE A BATH!  **¡BÁÑATE!**

Mueve la mano detrás de la cabeza como si estuvieras restregándote.

Squat, then stand up, pulling on invisible pajamas.

JAMMIES ON!  **¡PONTE EL PIJAMA!**

Agáchate y levántate como poniéndote un pantalón invisible.

Unfold hands like a book.

READ A BOOK!  **¡LEE UN LIBRO!**

Mueve las manos como si abrieras un libro.

Pull on an imaginary chain.

NIGHT-LIGHT ON!  **¡PRENDE LA LAMPARITA!**

Hala una cadenita imaginaria.

Hold hands beside head, then twist and turn.

TOSS AND TURN! **¡PARA ACÁ Y PARA ALLÁ!**

Con las manos a los lados de la cabeza, muévete para un lado y para el otro.

Run in place.

RUN AND HIDE!  **¡CORRE A ESCONDERTE!**

Haz como que corres.

Wag your finger back and forth.

NO MORE TRICKS!  **¡NO MÁS TRUCOS!**

Niega con el dedo.

Cross arms across chest and sway.

ALL TUCKED IN! **¡MÉTETE EN LA CAMA!**

Cruza las manos sobre el pecho y mécete.

Put hands together under your head.

OFF TO SLEEP! **¡A DORMIR!**

Pon las manos juntas debajo de la cabeza.